LAGRAN

S0-ACR-552

LAGRANGE COUNTY PUBLIC LIBRARY
BKM j MAR 101369
Margolin   The Good-Day Bunnies tooth

3 0477 0002 7817 0

OFFICIAL DISCARD

The Good-Day Bunnies

TOOTH DAY

LAGRANGE COUNTY LIBRARY

The Good-Day Bunnies

TOOTH DAY

By Harriet Margolin and Carol Nicklaus

A GOLDEN BOOK • NEW YORK

Western Publishing Company, Inc., Racine, Wisconsin 53404

Copyright © 1987 by Harriet Margolin. Illustrations copyright © 1987 by Carol Nicklaus. All rights reserved. Printed in the U.S.A. by Western Publishing Company, Inc. No part of this book may be reproduced or copied in any form without written permission from the publisher. GOLDEN®, GOLDEN & DESIGN®, and A GOLDEN BOOK® are trademarks of Western Publishing Company, Inc. Library of Congress Catalog Card Number: 86-82371
ISBN: 0-307-11648-4 / ISBN: 0-307-61648-7 (lib. bdg.)   A B C D E F G H I J

"Good day!" said Papa to everyone at the breakfast table. Papa had worked most of the night at the carrot-juice factory. "How is everyone this morning?"

Bumper looked up from his cereal and said, "I'm good, Papa."

Becky, Bumper's twin sister, stopped chewing her toast long enough to say, "I'm good too."

Baby Bonnie lifted her arms. She wanted to get out of her high chair and sit on her daddy's lap. Papa picked her up for a minute, then put her back in her own seat.

"Bumper, eat your toast," Grandma said.

"But I can't bite into it," answered Bumper. "My tooth is loose."

"It is not!" yelled Becky. "You're making it up. I know you are, because we're twins and my tooth's not loose."

"It's loose!" Bumper insisted. "Look at it move!"

Bumper wiggled his front tooth for everyone to see.

"Yuck!" said Becky.

"Well, what can a little child with a loose tooth eat for breakfast?" asked Mama. "What's soft enough?"

"Ice cream!" answered Bumper immediately.

"You can't have ice cream for breakfast," said Mama. "How about an egg?"

"No egg!" said Bumper. "I'll eat my toast."

Bumper took a big bite.

And guess what! Bumper's loose tooth came out!

"What should I do now?" Bumper asked.

Grandma answered first. "You should take your tooth out of the toast!"

Papa added, "Go to the sink and rinse out your mouth. And you can also wash off the tooth. But be careful not to wash it down the drain."

After he rinsed, Bumper put his tongue where his tooth used to be. Then he announced, "I have a hole in my mouth."

"Don't worry about it," said Mama. "The hole will soon fill up with another tooth, even bigger and stronger than the one you just lost."

Mama kissed Bumper.
Grandma kissed Bumper.
Papa kissed Bumper.
They all smiled and told him losing his first tooth was something to feel good about.

Becky was upset.

Everyone was making a big fuss over Bumper. Besides, when she pushed at her teeth with her tongue, not one moved. Not even a little. Bumper would probably get something from the tooth fairy, and there would be nothing for her!

Becky ran out of the kitchen even before she was excused.

Bumper ran after Becky. He wanted to show her his tooth. And then he wanted to put it under his pillow before it was time to leave for school.

"Becky! Becky!" he shouted. "Don't be mad. Your tooth will fall out soon!"

Becky didn't answer. She just picked up her school bag and headed for the door.

Soon Grandma called from downstairs, "Let's go, twins!
The bus is here!"

Becky and Bumper hurried outside. Mama followed.
She was on her way to work.

"Good-bye," Mama said. "Have a good day!"

"I will," said Bumper.

"I won't," thought Becky.

Now the house was quiet. Papa went to his bedroom for a nap.

"What should we do today?" Grandma asked Bonnie.

Bonnie walked over to the kitchen counter. She pointed to the mixing bowls.

Bonnie wanted Grandma to bake cookies. And she wanted to help her.

Grandma put everything on the kitchen table—flour, sugar, eggs, and butter; bowls and beaters, spoons and spatulas.

Bonnie sifted and Bonnie stirred.

Bonnie poured and Bonnie mixed.

Grandma dropped the batter onto the cookie sheet, one spoonful at a time.

When the cookies were just right, Grandma took them out of the oven and put them on a plate to cool.
Then she said, "It's time for your nap, Bonnie."

Now it was "Grandma's time"—time for Grandma to do whatever pleased her. She went to the living room to practice the violin.

Grandma was a good fiddler. She liked to make pretty music. Playing made her feel good inside.

Grandma played some slow songs, then some fast ones. She tapped her foot to keep the rhythm. Grandma's feet danced when she played.

Before Grandma knew it, Bonnie was calling.
Grandma took Bonnie out of her crib.

"Let's go downstairs and see if our cookies are ready for Becky and Bumper," Grandma said to Bonnie as she took her by the hand.

Bumper and Becky were coming up the path by the time Grandma and Bonnie got downstairs.

They came inside, dropped their school bags in the hall, and headed for the kitchen. They found the cookies all ready on the kitchen table.

"Here!" said Bonnie, handing each of them one cookie.
"Who made these?" Bumper asked.
Bonnie grinned from ear to ear. "Me!" she shouted.
"Well, they look good," said Bumper.

Becky and Bumper sat down for glasses of milk.

Becky bit hard into her cookie, hoping her tooth would fall out just like Bumper's. But it didn't—even though Becky bit and chewed as hard as she could.

"Do you believe in the tooth fairy?" Bumper asked.

"Yup!" Becky answered. "I believe if you leave your tooth in an envelope under your pillow, someone will come, take the tooth, and leave a present instead."

"What kind of present?"

"I think tooth fairies leave whatever they want, but mostly it's money," said Becky.

"How much do you think?"

"A quarter…but you'll probably only get a nickel."

"You're mean," answered Bumper. "I'm going upstairs to check under my pillow."
Bumper ran up the stairs.
Becky followed close behind.

Bumper ran right to his bed and shouted, "The tooth fairy's been here! And she left an envelope under my pillow!"

Bumper tore open the lumpy envelope and smiled as he read the message:

"Loose tooth...wiggly tooth...a bite of toast...and tooth falls out! Here is a shiny new quarter from me.
Hope this has been a good day!
                              Love,
                              The Tooth Fairy
P.S. I thought you would want to save your tooth for a while, so I'm returning it to you."

Becky was sitting on her bed, looking miserable. But something made her check under her pillow.

"There's an envelope under my pillow too!" she yelled across the room. "And it's lumpy!"

Becky ripped open the envelope. Inside she found a letter and a shiny new quarter.

"What did the tooth fairy tell you?" Bumper asked.

Becky read, "'Your tooth will come out when it's ready! And not one minute sooner. In the meantime, make every day a good day.'"

"Let's go thank the tooth fairy!" they both said together.
And that's just what Bumper and Becky did!